MW00815638

In the Time of Shimmer and Light

To Aiden

Love + peace

P. Eche 2018

To Lee, my beautiful and smart
peacock of a wife.

All paintings are acrylic on masonite

http://ulpress.org
University of Louisiana at Lafayette Press
P.O. Box 43558
Lafayette, LA 70504-3558

Printed on acid-free paper in the United States
Library of Congress Cataloging-in-Publication Data

Names: Schexnayder, Paul, author, illustrator.
Title: In the time of Shimmer and Light / Paul Schexnayder.
Description: Lafayette, LA : University of Louisiana at Lafayette Press,
    2018. | Summary: Queen Ida Peacock, Tin Toy Hare, and Sir Galatoir Gator
    all want the same glistening object, which becomes both the cause of, and
    cure for, their island's gloom.
Identifiers: LCCN 2018023732 | ISBN 9781946160294 (alk. paper)
Subjects: | CYAC: Lost and found possessions--Fiction. | Greed--Fiction. |
    Peacocks--Fiction. | Hares--Fiction. | Alligators--Fiction. |
    Trees--Fiction. | Islands--Fiction.
Classification: LCC PZ7.1.S33614 Is 2018 | DDC [E]--dc23
LC record available at https://lccn.loc.gov/2018023732

In the Time of Shimmer and Light

Paul Schexnayder

2018

University of Louisiana at Lafayette Press

Way back when, in the Time of Shimmer and Light, Queen Ida Peacock, Tin Toy Hare, and Sir Galatoire Gator all lived together on a happy island home.

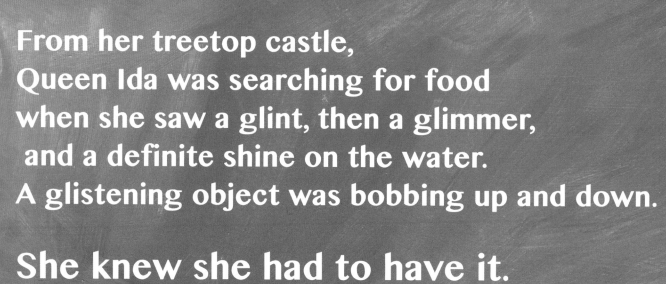

From her treetop castle,
Queen Ida was searching for food
when she saw a glint, then a glimmer,
and a definite shine on the water.
A glistening object was bobbing up and down.

She knew she had to have it.

After plucking it off the water,
she quickly flew back home.

Tin Toy Hare was strolling on the pink sandy beach when she looked up and saw Queen Ida swoop left and dive toward the water.

She saw a gleam dancing off a glittering gadget right before the Queen snatched it up.

Tin Toy Hare just knew she had to have it.

Sir Galatoire was half asleep under the shade of a very tall bamboo grove. A glow hit his eye and woke him up for good. He noticed the Queen rising from the water holding a fancy flickering item.

Sir Galatoire just knew he had to have it.

Back at her castle, Queen Ida placed the object on a bed of leaves.

"I am so proud of this joy and wonder I found.
I adore its slick and shiny surface
and the cap it wears is quite dapper."

She was mesmerized by it for hours
and almost missed her lunch plans.

The queen hurriedly covered
it with leaves and flew away.

Tin Toy Hare and
Sir Galatoire
made their way
to the base of the
Queen's castle.

WELCOME

Both greeted each
other with a curious
and cautious hello.

One rang the
doorbell as the other
pounded on the door.

Without wasting a
second, each said
in unison,

Tin Toy Hare
touched her nose
and was lifted to the
top of the tree.

Sir Galatoire
slapped his tail on the
ground and immediately
shot up to the top.

Not seeing the Queen, both started digging around in the leaves for the dazzling doodad.

Sir Galatoire found it first but Tin Toy Hare grabbed it.

They
bumbled it,
and fumbled it,
and it tumbled
right
out
the
nest.

Down the tree they went to look for
the object. Without finding it, both
mumbled and grumbled angrily.

"Look what you did!"

they shouted at each other
and went on their separate ways.

A cloud of gloom and despair hung over the island. No one was speaking to each other, no one was happy, and no one seemed to care.

The Queen requests you & your family at her castle tomorrow at dusk

It seemed that Queen Ida was in a royal mess, but she had a plan.

She requested the entire Hare and Gator families to gather at the base of her castle.

Everyone was staring at a red boat that had a cloth covering something in the center of it.

Queen Ida told Tin Toy Hare to place the boat on Sir Galatoire's back and for all to walk toward the beach.

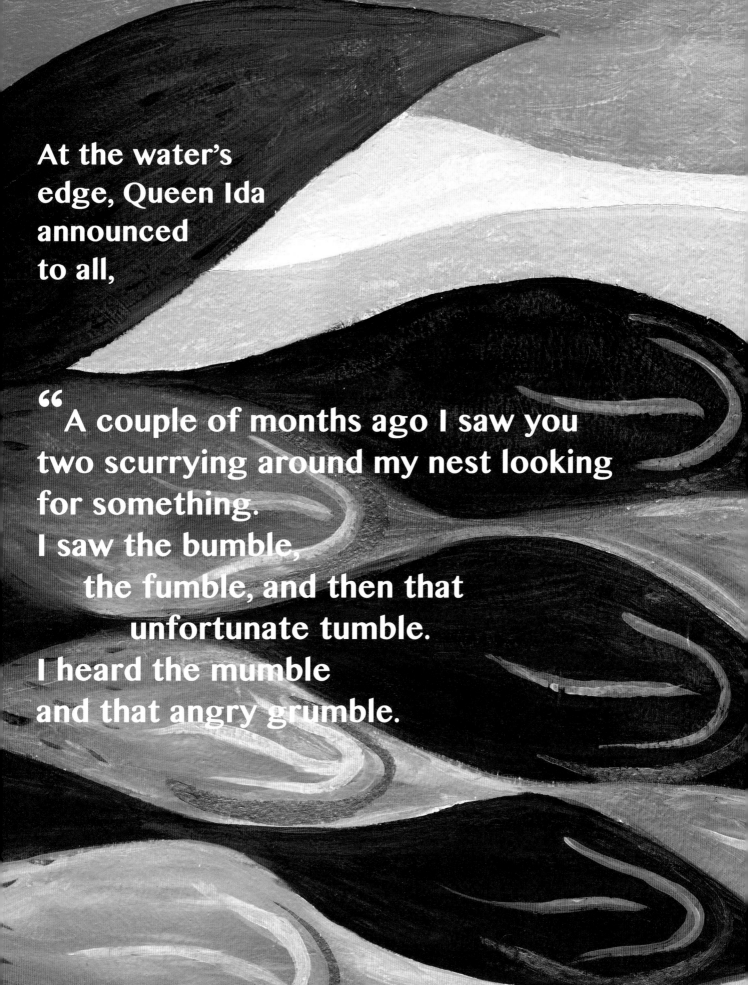

At the water's
edge, Queen Ida
announced
to all,

"A couple of months ago I saw you
two scurrying around my nest looking
for something.
I saw the bumble,
    the fumble, and then that
        unfortunate tumble.
I heard the mumble
and that angry grumble.

6"

"I observed that due to the heavy nature of the luminous object, the speed and velocity of the drop was quite impressive.

The force of the impact created a hole about 6 inches deep into the ground.

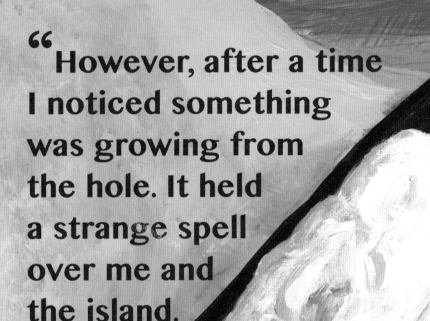

"However, after a time I noticed something was growing from the hole. It held a strange spell over me and the island.

I knew I must act quickly to restore peace and harmony so I dug it up today and placed it aboard this boat."

Queen Ida then pushed the boat into
the water and removed the cloth,
revealing the living specimen.

As it floated away under the moonlit
sky, everyone smiled and was sure
they saw a hint of a glint,
a shimmer of a glimmer,
and a definite shine
reflecting off a proud young sapling.

About the Author

A native of New Iberia, Louisiana, Paul Schexnayder earned his Bachelor of Fine Art degree from Louisiana State University. He has since worked as an artist, author/illustrator, and art teacher. Despite being colorblind, he is well known for his intensely colorful acrylic paintings, which often feature Louisiana themes, and which are as whimsical and poetic as they are mysterious and thought-provoking. Schexnayder is a member of the Society of Children's Book Writers and Illustrators, has illustrated over half a dozen children's books, and has been the official Louisiana artist of many state festivals and events. He owns an art gallery in his hometown of New Iberia, where he currently lives with his wife and three children. For more information about Paul and his work, visit his website at www.schex.com.